MOP RIDES THE WAVES OF LIFE

STORY BY JAIMAL YOGIS

ILLUSTRATED BY

MATTHEW ALLEN

✿ PLUM BLOSSOM BOOKS

BERKELEY, CALIFORNIA

PLUM BLOSSOM BOOKS

Plum Blossom Books, the children's imprint of Parallax Press, publishes books on mindfulness for young people and the grown-ups in their lives.

Parallax Press
P.O. Box 7355
Berkeley, California 94707
parallax.org

Story © 2020 Jaimal Yogis
Illustrations © 2020 Matthew Allen
Cover and interior design
by Debbie Berne

ISBN: 978-1-946764-60-7

1 2 3 4 5 / 23 22 21 20 19

Library of Congress Cataloging-in-Publication Data

Names: Yogis, Jaimal, author. | Allen, Matt, illustrator. | Parallax Press.
Title: Mop rides the waves of life : a story of mindfulness and surfing / story by Jaimal Yogis; illustrated by Matt Allen.
Description: Berkeley, California : Plum Blossom Books, the children's imprint of Parallax Press, 2020. | Audience: Ages 4-8 years
Identifiers: LCCN 2020000085 (print) | LCCN 2020000086 (ebook) | ISBN 9781946764607 (Hardcover) | ISBN 9781946764614 (eBook)
Subjects: LCSH: Surfing—Juvenile literature. | Mindfulness (Psychology)—Juvenile literature. | Surfing—Religious aspects.
Classification: LCC GV840.S8 Y64 2020 (print) | LCC GV840.S8 (ebook) | DDC 797.3/2—dc23
LC record available at https://lccn.loc.gov/2020000085
LC ebook record available at https://lccn.loc.gov/2020000086

MIX
Paper from responsible sources
FSC® C016245

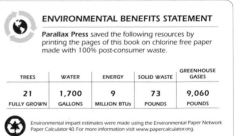

ENVIRONMENTAL BENEFITS STATEMENT

Parallax Press saved the following resources by printing the pages of this book on chlorine free paper made with 100% post-consumer waste.

TREES	WATER	ENERGY	SOLID WASTE	GREENHOUSE GASES
21	1,700	9	73	9,060
FULLY GROWN	GALLONS	MILLION BTUs	POUNDS	POUNDS

Environmental impact estimates were made using the Environmental Paper Network Paper Calculator 4.0. For more information visit www.papercalculator.org.

For Mom —J

For the kids who bring me so much joy:
Parker, Macie, Mikah, Ford, CJ, Cam,
Brooks, Brennan, and Bennett —M

Hi.
I'm Mop.

People call me Mop
because, well . . .
Yeah.

I love to **SURF**.

A lot lot lot lot lot lot lot lot lot lot!

I love to paddle.

I love to wait for just the right wave . . .

TO RIDE!

I like school too.

But on Monday Toby said I play four square like a baby.

So I **PUSHED** him in the sandbox.

I thought it would make me feel better.

It didn't.

On Tuesday, Izzy said I looked like a poodle.

"I like poodles!" I shouted later.

This was becoming a bad week.

On Wednesday Mom made me help her clean the van—even the moldy banana peel between the seats.

And on Thursday we ran out of my favorite cereal.

It was officially a **BAD** week.

But finally, after school, Mom took me surfing!
"Mop," Mom said. "You're a great surfer. But you
can learn to surf life, too."

"Surf life?" I laughed. "That sounds hokey."

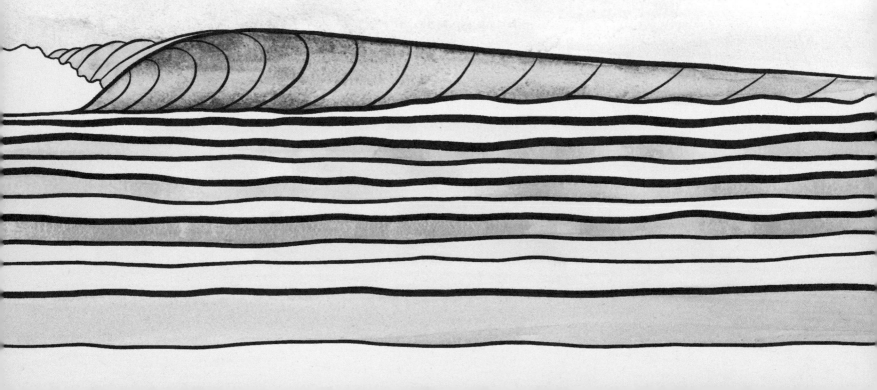

"Have you tried?" Mom smiled.

"Not exactly," I said.

"You start by feeling your breath go in and out like the tides. Breathing mindfully helps you notice the emotional waves inside."

"Feels like floating on my board," I said.

"So when you feel bad, don't be scared. Stormy waves are natural."

"Just breathe and let those waves pass. Like the ocean, your mind is always changing."

"And if a scary-grouchy-sad-mad wave catches you in its grip, it's okay. Falling is the best way to learn."

"When happy feelings come, enjoy them."

"But when happy feelings go, smile and keep paddling. There are always more good waves coming."

"I get it, Mom," I said. "Ride the good waves, and let the bad ones cruise by."

"That's right, Mop," Mom said.

After the surf, Friday started out cool. Mrs. Grickle said my drawing of farm animals on Mars was "extremely creative!"

Then we played sharks and minnows, and Sammy and I were the last minnows in the whole class.

I wasn't just surfing Friday.

I was **SHREDDING** it.

Until I got a math problem wrong and Izzy shouted: "Mop looks like Albert Einstein! But he's not smart."

Everyone laughed.

I wanted to break something.

I wanted to crawl in a hole and sob.

But I didn't.

I felt my breathing, in and out like the tides.

I remembered angry waves are natural.

I tried to see the anger as a wave.

I saw I had a choice.

I still felt a little bad. But I knew bad wouldn't last.

"I'm not Einstein," I told Izzy. "I'm just Mop. And I'm still learning."

At recess, Izzy said she was sorry for teasing me. I felt better right away.

I realized I wanted to say I was sorry to Toby. I still felt bad about pushing him.

He said he was sorry, too, and we all laughed and played four square with Sammy.

At the end of the day, I was full of all kinds of good feelings to ride . . .

all the way back to the beach!